dear
sister

Also by Alison McGhee

Firefly Hollow

Little Boy

Maybe a Fox

Pablo and Birdy

So Many Days

Someday

Star Bright

What I Leave Behind

dear sister

by Alison McGhee
illustrated by Joe Bluhm

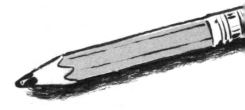

A Caitlyn Dlouhy Book

atheneum

Atheneum Books for Young Readers
New York   London   Toronto   Sydney   New Delhi

ATHENEUM BOOKS FOR YOUNG READERS
An imprint of Simon & Schuster Children's Publishing Division
1230 Avenue of the Americas, New York, New York 10020

Text copyright © 2018 by Alison McGhee
Illustrations copyright © 2018 by Joe Bluhm

ATHENEUM BOOKS FOR YOUNG READERS is a registered trademark of Simon & Schuster, Inc.
Atheneum logo is a trademark of Simon & Schuster, Inc.
For information about special discounts for bulk purchases, please contact Simon & Schuster Special
Sales at 1-866-506-1949 or business@simonandschuster.com.
The Simon & Schuster Speakers Bureau can bring authors to your live event.
For more information or to book an event, contact the Simon & Schuster Speakers Bureau
at 1-866-248-3049 or visit our website at www.simonspeakers.com.
Book design by Sonia Chaghatzbanian and Joe Bluhm
The text for this book was hand-lettered.
The illustrations for this book were rendered in mixed media.
Manufactured in the United States of America
0818 FFG
First Edition
2 4 6 8 10 9 7 5 3 1
Library of Congress Cataloging-in-Publication Data
Names: McGhee, Alison, 1960– author.
Title: Dear Sister / Alison McGhee.
Description: First edition. | New York : Atheneum, [2018] | "A Caitlyn Dlouhy Book." | Summary: Brother
chronicles life with his frequently annoying Sister, from the time she is born until she is ten and he leaves
for college, through a series of letters and drawings.
Identifiers: LCCN 2017036049 | ISBN 9781481451420 (hardcover) | ISBN 9781481451444 (eBook)
Subjects: | CYAC: Brothers and sisters—Fiction. | Letters—Fiction. | Humorous stories.
Classification: LCC PZ7.M4784675 De 2018 | DDC [Fic]—dc23
LC record available at https://lccn.loc.gov/2017036049

To my hilarious, beloved brother, Doug
—A. M.

Our first child Betty was born while making this book.
Everything is now for her.
—J. B.

dear
sister

Dear Sister,

They told me to draw a
picture of you for your
baby book.

Here you go.

Even though it is not my fault that you look like this, they decided not to put my picture of you in your baby book.

Dear Sister,
They told me to write you a
Three Months Old note for
your baby book.

Here you go.

From,
Brother

PS: The reason I signed it
From is because I am not
sure I love you yet.

Time will tell.

PPS: It's not looking good so far.

Dear Sister,

In my school, they give everyone
a progress report twice a year.

Here's your half-year
progress report.

PROGRESS

Crying: Excellent

Diaper issues: Excellent

Poking brother in eye:
                    Excellent

Spitting up on brother:
                    Excellent

Pulling brother's hair: Excellent

Dear Sister,
They told me to make
you a card for your
first birthday.

Dear Sister,

  Here is a picture of you as a one-year-old for your baby book.

  Shot down again.

Just FYI, Joe liked it.

We put it up in the tree house.

Dear Sister,

Their question: Why do I only call you Sister? Because I had a good name picked out for you, that's why.

But did they listen to me?

Nope.

So Sister it is.

PS: Joe liked the name I picked out for you, too.

PPS: We would tell you what the name was but then you would love it so much and wish it was your name so much instead of the name you ended up with that you would cry even more than you cry now. Which is a TON.

PPPS: It's better for everyone this way.

dear sister,

Joe and I also have a special nickname for you, but it's classified information, which means we can't tell you what it is. If we did tell you, we'd have to lock you up forever.

Which might not be the **worst** idea in the world.

Dear Sister,

They told me to make a card for your second birthday and a drawing for your baby book.

Baby book baby book baby book baby book baby book baby book baby book Blah blah BLAH BLAH BLAH BLAH BLAH BABY BLAH BOOK.

~~Anywher~~ Anyway, here you go.

From,
Brother

dear sister,

You know that picture I drew
of me reading that book to you?

This is a picture of me
reading that same book to you
for the 763rd time.

Notice anything different?

Dear Sister,

Life was a lot less complicated before they brought you home.

Just sayin'.

From,

Brother

PS: I can't wait.

Dear Sister,

Joe and I sincerely apologize for teaching you to say all those inappropriate words.

Sincerely,
Brother

PS: The sincere apology above is a prepared statement that the wardens made us sign.

PPS: In our defense, who knew you would start shouting them in church?

I mean **church?**

Geez.

Dear Sister,

Repeat after me:

"There is no law that says my big brother has to read me the same book 99,999 times in a row."

Good. Now repeat after me again:

"But he does anyway. Why is that? Because he is the greatest brother in the history of the world."

PS: "The greatest, most bored brother in the history of the world."

PPS: Here is a picture I drew of you with a fake big brother who never gets bored reading that book to you. ~~like I do.~~

Happy Third Birthday to the Person Who Made Me a Big Brother.
(you)
From,
The Tormented Big Brother

Dear Sister,

In seven years, when I am a legal adult I will run away to live in a houseboat far from the world as we know it, and then I will be free from you. And until then I will not be free from you. So I have to get used to it, because this is what being a big brother is all about. I did not make these rules, but there are many, many other rules in life that will strike me as unfair, and I still have to live by all of them.

Or so the wardens have told me.

Many, many times.

PS: Eighteen cannot come soon enough.

dear sister,

Congratulations! According to the judges' calculations, your Cry Olympics scores place you in the top 3% of three-year-olds nationwide.

What?

It's a compliment!

The judge and his best friend have been unfairly imprisoned.

The judge is hungry.

Very hungry.

By peering through his cell's bars, he can see the wardens eating dinner with his sister while he languishes in his cell.

Dear Sisterish Person,

Here is a picture of my hands waving bye-bye to you, the way they will be doing when I run away to live in my houseboat far from the world as we know it.

PS: Joe is also waving bye-bye.

PS: The sincere apology on the previous page is a prepared statement that the wardens forced me to sign.

PPS: In my defense, no one else's little sister came running onto the court halfway through the first quarter, screaming MY BALL MY BALL MY BALL.

Dear Person Who Is Supposedly Related to Me,

Here is a picture of the book that I will no longer have to read to you ever again once I am living on my houseboat and catching fish and learning to surf.

A day that <u>cannot</u> come too soon.

Dear Sister,

Happy fourth birthday.

Here is your card. Here is
a picture for your baby book.

Ever hear the phrase
"Resistance is futile"?

dear sister,

Here is a picture of me in my prison cell doing one of my prison jobs, which is reading that book to you over and

ver
and
nd over
over and over and over
er and over and over and
and over and over
nd over and over and
over and over and over
and over and over and
over and over and over
r and over and over and.
nd over
ver

**AND
OVER.**

FOUR-YEAR PROGRESS REPORT

Whininess: World-class

Annoyingness: World-class

Afraid of the darkness: World-class

Continued refusal to eat lima beans
and getting your way even though
I don't like lima beans either:

TOTALLY UNFAIR

Dear ~~Tattletale~~ Sister,

Joe and I sincerely apologize to you for making you be our servant for the entire day until bedtime.

Sincerely,
Me and Joe

PS: The sincere apology above is a prepared statement that the wardens forced us to sign.

dear sister,

No, they are not fun.

No, they don't feel good.

No, you can't try them on.

No, I don't want to see the picture you made for me.

I said No. I don't want to see it.

Do you still not understand the meaning of **NO**?

Oh, WHATEVER.

What do I think?

What do you mean, what do I think? About what? Current politics? The State of the environment?

Oh, what do I think about your _drawing_?

Hmm.

Well.

It could be worse.
That's what I think.

Dear Person with Horrible Taste in Movies,

Joe and I sincerely apologize for pretending we didn't know you and the Annoying Tabitha yesterday.

Sincerely,
Brother

PS: The sincere apology on the previous page is a prepared statement that the wardens forced us to sign.

PPS: In our defense, no ~~kid~~ middle schooler wants to be seen at a movie like that.

PPPS: I mean, COME ON!

Dear Sister,

Happy Birthday to you
Happy Birthday to you
Happy Birthday, person who
doesn't know the meaning of
the word "privacy"
Happy fifth birthday to you.

From,
Brother

dear sister,

    No.

I do not want to read your book to you.
I do not want to play a game with you.
I do not want to watch a movie with you.
I do not want to do anything with you.

I do not want to do anything
with anyone.

Except Joe.

But I can't.

Because Joe is moving to Florida.

Dear Sister,

I got the card. Thank you.

But it does not help.

Nothing helps.

Dear Sister,

I got the candy. Thank you. Even if it is leftover from Halloween.

But candy doesn't help either.

The only thing that could help is if Joe were not moving to Florida. And Joe is still moving to Florida.

Dear Sister,
    Thank you for the drawing.
It's good.
    PS: Really good.

Dear Sister,

By the time you get this, you will have made it through your first morning of kindergarten.

And you will have found this note taped to your apple.

But because you don't know how to read, you will have no idea what it says.

Which means that I could have written something horrible, like "Dear Booger" or "Dear Tiny Poo."

But don't worry. I didn't. Not that you would know either way, because, reading. Which you don't know how to do.

Right at this very minute, I bet you're wondering what horrible means, aren't you? Seeing as it jumps right out from the page in these giant letters.

HORRIBLE.

All right, I'll tell you. Horrible is what it feels like to go your first day of eighth grade without Joe because he moved to Florida.

PS: Not that you would know.

There's this saying, "If a tree falls in a forest, and no one hears it, does it make a sound?"

That's what this note is like, except with reading.

Love,
Brother

PPS: Also, this is the first time I ever put "love" on one of these notes. But you don't know that, either.

Dear Sister,

Why am I grouchy, you ask?

Because.

Because why?

Because I used to think Joe living three blocks away was too far.

Boy, was I wrong. Nothing is the same anymore.

PS: Except you. You're the same.

PPS: Except not. Even you're different. A little.

Lima beans

me   you

FIVE-AND-THREE-QUARTERS-YEAR
PROGRESS REPORT

WHININESS:	Not quite as bad
ANNOYINGNESS:	Also not quite as bad
AFRAID OF THE DARKNESS:	Some things never change
CONTINUED REFUSAL TO EAT LIMA BEANS:	Inspirational!

Dear Sister,

Is Joe as good a friend as the Annoying Tabitha, you ask?

Is that even a question?

SHAKING

MY

HEAD.

Joe
(best)

Tabitha

1

(not
best)

Dear Sister,

Yes, I know you've grown another inch.

Yes, I do know what that means.

The good news: You're still too little to climb up.

The bad news: You're getting bigger.

Dear Sister,

What tattoo do I plan to get when I turn 18?

That's classified information.

I could tell you, but then I'd have to kill you. Wouldn't go over well with the wardens.

Dear Sister,
    Happy sixth birthday
to someone who is still obnoxious.

(But not quite as obnoxious
    as she used to be.)

(at least not struck by lightning)

dear sister,

    Can you come visit me on my
future ~~boat~~ houseboat, you ask?
    Your request, along with your
supporting materials will be taken into
consideration.

Dear Sister,

Will I come back sometimes to visit you when I am living on my houseboat, you ask?

It's a distant possibility.

We'll see how it goes.

Dear Sister,

Will you miss me when I'm living on my houseboat as much as I miss Joe right now, you ask?

Dear Sister,

What do you mean, I can't help you with your writing?

I always help you with your writing. What do you mean you can't tell me why?

What do you mean, it's your private business? And by the way, if you know what "private" means, why do you choose to ignore signs that say

PRIVATE ?

Oh, WHATEVER.

Dear Sister,

What do I think of your card?

What I think is that it could be worse.

Much worse.

PS: Now I see why you wouldn't let me help you with your writing.

Female Person!
Can you not see that
I am TRYING to SLEEP?!

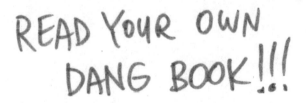

READ YOUR OWN
DANG BOOK!!!

Dear Female Person,

Why should I apologize to you for referring to you as a "female person"?

Are you not (a) female and (b) a person?

PS: Wait, are you trying to tell me that you are not actually a person?

This would explain a great many things, especially back in the early days.

Dear Sister,

    I sincerely apologize for referring to you at the dinner table as my ball and chain.

Sincerely,
Brother

PS: The sincere apology above is a prepared statement that the wardens forced me to sign.

PPS: In my defense, a 14-year-old high school student should not have to take his little sister to the playground.

Although, I suppose it could be worse.

Dear Sister,

Yes, it was a BAD day.

NO, something didn't go wrong at school, **MANY** things went wrong.

- There was the retainer incident.

- There was the falling-off-the-bleachers incident.

- There was the ask-Sariya-to-Homecoming-Dance rejection incident.

Too many incidents.

No, I don't want to talk about it.
Yes, if Joe were here, I would talk to him.

But Joe isn't here.

NO, I don't want to go up in the tree house.

Yes, if Joe were here, we would go up in the tree house.

But Joe isn't here.

No, you can't help me.

Why not? Because you are not Joe.

For the last time,
Joe ISN'T HERE.

So STOP ASKING
ME
QUESTIONS.

Dear Female Who May or May not
be a Person but Who Probably is,

Happy Seventh Birthday.

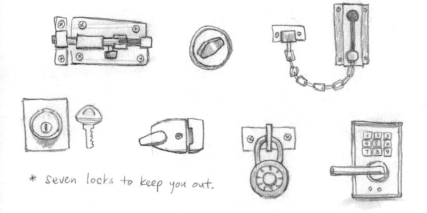

* seven locks to keep you out.

Yes, yes, yes, yes, yes, yes yes yes
yes, I will read your book to
you when you go to bed.

Ever hear the phrase, "pick
your battles"?

Yeah.

You!
GIRL PERSON!
HOUSE RESIDENT!

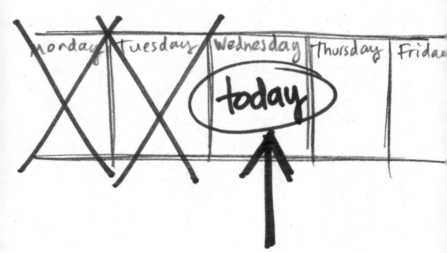

It's not your birthday anymore!

You are seven! You know how to read!

SO. READ. YOUR. OWN. DANG. BOOK.

Dear Sister,

When can you come up in my tree house, you ask?

My answer remains the same as in years past:

When the _time_ is right.

dear Sister,

When can you borrow my telescope, you ask?

— See above response. —

Dear Sister,

When can you borrow my paints, you ask?

⟶ See above response. ⟵

dear sister,

When can you read my notebook,
you ask?

Never.

Dear ~~Sister~~ House Resident Who Just
Told Me That She Would Not
Ever Visit Me When I'm
Living on my Stupid
Houseboat,

FINE.

Dear Younger, Smaller, Slower Person
Who Just Slammed the Door to
Her Room,

Try to understand.
Sometimes I just
Want

TO

GO

FAST.

Dear Sister,
    Happy Eighth birthday.
    I will read your book to you
when you go to bed tonight. DUH.

    Also:

THIS COUPON GOOD FOR
ONE VISIT TO
OLDER BROTHER'S HOUSE-
BOAT SOMETIME IN THE
                    DISTANT
                    FUTURE.

Welcome

PS: Please note: NO visitors will be allowed onto the houseboat without an original coupon and the proper photo identification.

Dear Fellow House Resident,

Here is a picture of you this afternoon when you finally, finally, finally read that book to yourself.

PS: FREE AT LAST.

dear sister,

Don't be so dramatic. It's only for a week. seven days. 1/52 of a year.

Plus, if the Annoying Tabitha had moved to Florida and you hadn't seen her in three years, wouldn't you want to go visit, too?

one tiny short week (that clearly won't be long enough)

I never get nearly enough presents

Summer starts

You get way too many presents again, just for showing up.

school starts

thanksgiving

one year

Spring break

you get way too many presents.

we see each other ALL the Time!

Stupid valentine's day

new year

You cannot come.

You will survive.

Yes, I know I will be missing your birthday.
Yes, I know that makes you sad.

It kind of makes me sad too.

But keep that to yourself. That's classified information.

Dear Sister,

    Of course it wasn't the same without me.

    I mean, the wardens try. You have to give them that.

    But wardens are wardens, and brothers are brothers, and that's the way it is.

dear sister,

   Yes, it was a good trip.

   Except not really.

   No, I can't explain it. You wouldn't understand.

Could you please stop bugging me?

   Yes, we're still friends, but **no,** we're not best friends.

   Yes, I miss him, and **no,** that's not the problem.

   You're too little to understand the problem, which is that I miss the old Joe and the old me and the old way it used to be.

Everything is different now.

Everything changes.

Okay, not everything.

Dear Sister,
   I'm sorry your stomach hurts.

PS: I mean it.

BROTHERS

Dear Sister,

They should let brothers stay in the hospital when their sisters have appendicitis.

PS: Tell you what, when you come home from the hospital, I will be your servant for one entire day until bedtime.

Dear Sister,

Please feel better soon.

Please please please please
please please please please please
please please please please
please please please please
please please please please
please please please please
please please please please
please please please please
please please please
please please please
please please please please

please please please
please please please
please please please

please please.

from the brother who
loves you.

At least sometimes.

Dear Sister Who Is Finally Home,

Repeat after me:

"I will not make rash promises, the way my big brother did when he promised to be my servant for one entire day until bedtime."

Whatever,
Brother

dear sister,

Yeah, going to camp can be scary. I don't blame you. I was scared, too.

But just think of all the cool presents you can make for me when you get there.

Dear Sister,

By the time you get this, you will already be in your cabin at camp.

And since you FINALLY know how to read, you will be able to follow this simple command:

Look in the bottom of your sleeping bag.

Love,
Brother

Dear Sister,

The GIFT REVIEW BOARD has received your recent camp offerings and graded them on a scale of 1-10 as follows:

PICTURE:	**7.3**
FEATHER:	**6.4**
BIRCH BARK:	**8.1**
LANYARD:	**9**

The GIFT REVIEW BOARD encourages you to keep working. Future offerings will be graciously accepted.

Love,
Brother.

PS: I miss you, too.

Dear Sister,

NO, I will not be applying to the University of Kathmandu.

I only said that because you would not stop singing that <u>horrible</u> song in my face over and over, and Kathmandu is the farthest-away place I could think of.

dear sister,

Why did I change my mind about living on a houseboat far from the world as we know it?

I didn't.

I just decided to go to college first.

Dear Sister,

Will you be allowed to climb up into my tree house when you're old and have gray hair and walk with a cane, you ask?

POSSIBLY.

If you play your cards right.

DOUBLE-DIGIT PROGRESS REPORT

WHINESS:	Could be worse.
ANNOYINGNESS:	Could be worse.
AFRAID OF THE DARKNESS:	Some things never change.
CONTINUED REFUSAL TO EAT LIMA BEANS:	SOLIDARITY

Dear Sister,

How will you survive when it's just you and the wardens, you ask?

The coupon below will help.

Also, the wardens aren't that bad. I had eight years alone with them before you showed up, and look how good I turned out.

dear sister,
When am I going to get my tattoo, you ask?
When I go to college.
dear sister,
Will my tattoo be a picture of you, you ask?
It will NOT.

dear sister,
Will my tattoo be
a picture of Joe,
you ask?

It will not.

dear sister,
Do I still miss Joe
after all this time,
you ask?   Yes.

Some things you
never stop missing.

Dear Sister,

When will I let you see my tattoo, you ask?

When the time is right.

Dear Sister,
    When am I leaving,
you ask?

        Soon.

Very soon.

Dear Sister,

I know.

I'm kinda going to miss you, too.

Dear Wardens,

After a decade of forced consumption, we declare an official boycott of the gross "food" you call lima beans.

SOLIDARITY

Dear Sister,
    Yes.
    Everything is different now.
    Everything changes.
    Almost everything.

Dear Sister,

By the time you read this, I will be at college.

Your mission, should you choose to accept it:

① Go look at the tree house.

(2) Go look on my desk.

③ And look under your pillow, too.

PS: I got my tattoo.

Alison McGhee

is the critically acclaimed author of the *New York Times* bestseller *Someday*, as well as *What I Leave Behind*, *Pablo and Birdy*, *Maybe a Fox*, Christopher Award–winning *Firefly Hollow*, *Little Boy*, *So Many Days*, and *Star Bright*, to name a few. She splits her time between Minneapolis, Minnesota, and Laguna Beach, California. You can visit her at alisonmcghee.com.

Joe Bluhm

is an Academy Award–winning artist who co-illustrated William Joyce's *New York Times* bestseller, *The Fantastic Flying Books of Mr. Morris Lessmore*, and is the illustrator of *The Magician's Secret*. He's also an animation art director, character designer, and story artist. Joe currently lives in Louisiana with his wife, daughter, and their plethora of dogs (plus one cat). Visit him at joebluhm.com.